I0593226

The Lustful Leprechaun

Helen Walton

Walton House Publishing

Contents

A Short Story

♥

I SWUNG MY FULL suitcase off the bed with my left hand since my right arm was still in a cast from the motorbike accident. Dropping it to the floor with a loud clunk, I placed my hand on my hip.

"I can't believe you're not coming home with me for the Saint Patrick's Day celebrations," I said. "Who'll wear the tiny leprechaun dress with me now?"

My sister, Hazel, laughed.

"Olive, I'll wear my costume here and we'll FaceTime. It'll be like I was there."

"Not the same." I flicked my long hair over my shoulder.

"Admit it, you're nervous about bumping into Tate."

"I am not," I said with a huff, dropping my hand and yanking the handle out of the suitcase. "I couldn't care less about seeing Tate. In fact, I hope I see him so I can rub it in his face how well I'm doing in Georgia acting in the television show."

Hazel twirled her hair around her finger. "Mmm hmm."

"What's that supposed to mean?"

"Your acting is good. You know that, but you're not fooling me."

I sighed and sunk onto the edge of the mattress. Every little hurt I held inside from Tate not coming to Georgia with me reared to the surface. If he loved me as much as he said he did, then why hadn't he moved here with me knowing I had a role lined up in a television show? This was my dream career. Famous actress. Albeit in a television show. One day, I'd be a star on the big screen in Hollywood. So what if he'd caught a big break himself after all his minor roles and would star in a movie this year? I wasn't jealous at all. Neither did I still have feelings for him.

A loud knock echoed through the front door and my lies. Hazel squealed and ran for the door. I gathered myself, stood, and dragged my bag out of my bedroom to the lounge room. Hazel and her boyfriend Valentine, who was also my co-star, were locking lips in a scorching kiss.

I cleared my throat, but that didn't stop them.

"All right, break it up or I'll miss my plane."

Hazel wriggled out of Valentine's arms and threw me a rueful grin. I didn't mind. After all, I'd set the pair up. I couldn't have done a better job of it even if I said so myself when they hooked up on Valentine's Day and hadn't been apart since.

"Here, let me take your bag," Valentine said, eyeing my cast and taking the handle from me. Then he opened the front door.

I trundled behind him. Hazel locked the door and caught up to me.

"This works out so well with you leaving for a week and my friend Candy and her boyfriend Devin coming for a visit from Australia. What are the odds your planes would arrive and depart at the same time, too?"

"Luck sure is shining on you here." I threaded my arm through hers.

"You'll say hello to Mom and Dad for me, won't you?"

"Of course."

We both missed our parents but acting was our calling. From the time we could talk, we both said we wanted to be stars and have our names on the Hollywood Walk of Fame. One day we'd both have that. Dreams came true if you worked hard enough for them. We walked out of our apartment building into the cool, early morning breeze. The gust blew the short hem of my skirt up around my legs almost over my bottom, like one of those Marilyn Monroe moments. I struggled with the fabric as a driver took my bag from Valentine and placed it in the trunk of the sedate black sedan. Without waiting for him to open the car door, I dove inside the car, grateful for the warm interior.

I smoothed my windswept hair, opened my purse, and took out the compact, checking my reflection in the mirror.

Hazel and Valentine climbed into the car and buckled their seatbelts. It was a tad squishy with the three of us in the back, but I bet Hazel didn't mind being shoved up against Valentine. Valentine grinned at me over Hazel's head, and I smiled back. He'd always been a good friend to me since we started filming the show. It's how I recognized he'd be perfect for my sister.

The ride to the airport flashed by. My nerves started making my palms sweat the closer we got. It wasn't the flying I was worried about. It was seeing Tate. No matter how much I played it off, I still loved him.

Pity he didn't love me.

The car stopped at the drop-off point. I kissed Hazel on the cheek and climbed out of the car.

"Olive," she said, leaning out of the car.

"Yeah?"

"I... well... you and Tate, you should talk. You know... never mind. Have fun!" She slammed the door closed.

As if I wanted to talk to Tate. The driver opened the boot and handed me my suitcase. I yanked the handle up, dragging it through the airport with my sweaty palms, despondent heart, and less than an enthusiastic desire to go home for the holiday.

"Mom, Dad." I greeted my parents with kisses on their cheeks at the airport.

They kissed me back, then embraced me in a group hug and fussed over the cast on my arm. This was nice after the plane ride from hell. Turbulence meant the seatbelt sign stayed on the entire flight and I didn't get one drink.

"How was your flight?" Dad asked.

"Don't ask." I grimaced.

"Well, you can come home and eat all the cookies you want," Mom said.

"You made a cookie table for Saint Patrick's Day?"

"I did." She nodded.

"Any excuse to make cookies," Dad said, taking my suitcase and leading me to the car.

We all climbed into his familiar car and trundled back home. I breathed deeply. Pittsburgh would always be home. My parents and their house would always be home, too.

"How's your sister?"

"She's good."

"Hazel sounds happy with that co-star of yours," Dad said.

"She is."

"Pity they couldn't come for tomorrow."

"Yeah." I rested my head back on the seat.

"You okay, sunshine? Is your broken arm giving you problems?"

"I'm fine, Dad." I smiled, but it stretched my lips more like a grimace. The cast on my arm was more a hindrance than anything else.

Mom frowned at me over her shoulder, and Dad flicked a concerned gaze at me in the rearview mirror. I perked up as my childhood home came into view. Familiarity and cookies. What more could a woman want?

Love.

I bit back that notion.

What was I so sad about? I had a fantastic career. A family who loved me, and a home I would always come home to.

Still, it felt like something, or should I say, someone, was missing.

"Look at you!" Hazel said over the phone, face timing me while dressed in her skimpy leprechaun outfit.

A woman's face decorated in green paint popped into view. "Hi. I'm Candy."

"Hi, Candy. I've heard a lot about you."

"Same." She grinned. "I can't wait to meet you in person when you get back."

A man's face, covered in green paint, appeared next to hers. Then they were gone, and it was me and Hazel staring at each other.

"I should let you go."

"Don't be like that," Hazel said.

"I'm not." For the billionth time, I checked the ribbons on my corset. "I need to head out, anyway. If I stay here and eat any more cookies, I'll be sick or the size of a house."

"Are you going to the Bighorn Bar?"

"I'm not sure yet."

"Don't lie, Olive. You're going there in that skimpy costume to rub his nose in it."

I grinned. "Think it'll work?"

"Knowing how Tate feels about you, you could turn up in a curtain and you'd still be rubbing his nose in it."

I laughed, trying to brush away the stupid race in my heart.

"Talk to you later."

"Bye." She waved like a lunatic as I ended the call.

With one last look in the mirror, I left my childhood bedroom. The room generated so many memories for me and Tate. My teenage crush, I'd set out to have him as mine. I had until the day we graduated from acting school. He loved me so much I believed he would follow me. I'd thought wrong. The breakup had been ugly. Tears and tantrums. Fights and sex. So much sex, like we were trying to keep ourselves from realizing we were over.

I walked into the lounge room. Even the sofa held memories of make-out sessions and the first time Tate had made it to third base with me. I needed green beer. Lots and lots of green Saint Patrick's Day beer.

"I'll see you both later. I'm going out," I said to my parents, who were on the back patio with their friends having their own celebrations.

Mom poked her head through the door. "Do you want your father to drive you?"

"No, thanks, I'll walk."

"Be careful," Mom said, even though she was a little tipsy already, and it was only midafternoon.

I waved, grabbed my coat from the rack, and ducked out the front door. The air was extra icy against my cheeks. I shoved my arm into the thick sleeve of my coat, tucked my broken arm around my waist, and buttoned up the coat to the top, even though it now covered my sexy costume. I couldn't make Tate regret breaking up with me if I froze before I saw him.

My high heels slid on the icy pavement as I made my way to the local pub. A crowd had already formed, and people were spilling out onto the street in front of the Bighorn Bar. I shoved my way inside. The heat of so many bodies hit me in an instant and I unbuttoned my coat as I made my way to the bar and the frothy goodness of green beer. A cheer rippled through the crowd. I ducked my head, thinking it was for me, but when no one rushed me asking for autographs, I glanced up. A crowd had formed to the side of the bar furthest away from me. I shrugged out of my coat, placed it on a bar stool, and enjoyed my good luck. The bar was now half empty so I could order.

Three bartenders rushed over to me, knocking each other in their haste to get to me first. Now, this is what I imagined would happen when people recognized me from my famous television show.

"What can I get you, Miss Sanchez?" The tallest and broadest of the three men asked me, having won out on getting to me first by sheer body mass.

"She'll have a green beer," Tate said. "Put it on my tab."

His deep voice ghosted over me from behind. I counted to three before turning around. Nothing could have prepared me for the way he looked. Tate had always been the most gorgeous boy in school. He'd grown into a stunning young man while we'd been dating, but now. Now he was broad and muscular, too. My damn hormones exploded into overdrive.

"Here you go, Miss Sanchez," the bartender said.

Turning back around, I took a deep breath to steady my nerves. I didn't mean for my body to still lust after him, but it did. Deep inside, my heart pounded against my ribs. Even that still lusted after him. The bartender gave me googly eyes. I spun back around before he imagined I liked him because I was staring at him for so long. He didn't realize I was just keeping my back to Tate.

"Thanks, Tate." I sipped the beer and avoided looking him in the eyes.

"How have you been, Olive?"

"Good. Great." I flicked back my hair and took another sip of beer, still avoiding looking directly at him. "And you?"

"Even with a broken arm?" He chuckled. The husky sound sent my pulse racing even harder, but then his warm finger swiped across the top of my lip. "You had a little foam."

My gaze followed the motion of his finger to his mouth. His tongue flicked out to lick the tip of his finger. My body flooded with instant arousal. The things Tate used to do to me with his tongue flashed through my mind, and my body remembered how talented he was with it. Heat worked its way through my body. Thankfully, I wasn't the sort of person to blush, but I needed away from him now. This wasn't how our meeting was supposed to go. I was meant to be in control of this meeting. Cool. Calm. Collected. As the saying went. I was anything but.

"I... ah... need the restroom." With that, I strode past him, spilling the beer over my hand in my haste to get away.

Squeezing through the crowd, I gave up trying to hang onto my beer and dumped the half-empty mug on a table as I walked past one. I made it to the hallway with the bathrooms, but there were lines, and I couldn't stand still. Every nerve ending in my body was alive.

I hadn't experienced this for so long I'd forgotten what it was like when Tate and I were together. No one had ever made me feel so much from so little like him.

"Olive, wait up," Tate said.

I peered over my shoulder as he shoved his way through the crowd to get to me. Even that made my heart stutter and race. The frantic way he stormed through the throng of people and the determination on his face made me pause. The people in the toilet line stared. Some even whipped out their phones and snapped photos.

"What do you want Tate?"

"I—"

A restroom door opened, and a man stepped out. Tate grabbed the door with one hand and my hand with the other. Before I knew it, he'd locked us in the bathroom.

"What are you doing?"

"I don't know. I thought." He ran a hand through his burnished brown hair. "I can't. I don't."

"You're not making any sense." I scowled. "Did you get hit in the head or something? Because you used to talk in full sentences."

He laughed. His deep green eyes landed on my face. I smirked back at him. He took a step toward me. My heart stuttered. Another step closer and we were standing as close as two people could without touching. Our warm breaths mingled. His chest heaved as much as mine. The air rippled with the same sexual tension we'd always experienced. His gaze flickered down to my lips and back up to my eyes. I wet my lips with my tongue. His gaze dropped again.

Then we were in each other's arms. Mouths fused in a hungry kiss. His tongue thrust into my mouth as his hands slid into my hair and he tugged the long strands, sending shivers dancing down my spine. I caressed his back with urgent hands, tugging at his shirt, cursing the awkwardness of the cast on my arm. He paused, kissing me long enough to peel off his jacket and yank the offending green garment over his head, and dropped them on the floor. The split-second glance I got at his chest was enough to make me drool and clench my thighs together. Tate dropped to his knees, lifted my skirt, and slid my thong to the side. He licked me hard and fast, sliding his tongue over my sensitive clit and then burying his tongue deep inside me over and over until my hips bucked into his face to the same fast rhythm he'd set. My legs shook as every muscle in my body tightened with pleasure. Tate's tongue swirled around my clit in one long languid caress that had me seeing stars and falling over the edge into an orgasm that shook my soul.

But Tate always had.

"Tate." I gasped, out of breath.

"Later." He grunted, standing, and picking me up by the waist.

He balanced my butt on the edge of the sink, slid his zipper down on the green pants, and released his enormous erection. How I'd missed the sight of him. The feel of him. Everything. He spread my thighs and eased into me. One slow inch at a time until he was all the way home.

Home.

This was what I'd been missing.

Tate was my home, too.

A deep sigh left my lungs. Tate cupped my face in his hands and searched my eyes with his. Whatever he glimpsed there made him kiss me with so much emotion, my inner muscles clamped around him. He rocked into me, a long slow slide in and out with his hard cock teasing me back to the peak of pleasure once more. This time, the ride was slow and sensual. I slid my hands to his back and drew him closer, wishing I didn't have the costume still on, so I'd experience the warmth of his skin against mine. His hands slid to the top of my corset and tugged the ribbons loose. He popped one breast free, then the other, and lowered his mouth to my eager nipples. Tate licked and sucked each nipple, sending pleasure shooting from my breasts to my core. Each tug carried me closer to orgasm. I hooked my legs around his hips.

"Are you still on birth control?" he asked with a raggedness to his voice that told me he was close to release.

"Yes."

"I need to fill you up, babe. Tell me you want that, too."

I sucked in a ragged breath. "Yes."

He dropped his head to my neck and kissed my collarbone. "I've missed you."

I clung to him tighter, as though holding onto him would keep him with me, and whispered, "I've missed you too."

He slid in and out, then ground his hips in a circular motion. "I can't hold out much longer, babe. Come with me."

Pleasure tightened my muscles and my heart raced so hard I thought I might pass out. Tate transported me to the brink of ecstasy and drove me over the edge. He came with me in a long, shuddering orgasm, his shoulders heaving as his hips jerked forward while his cock filled me up with his release. I floated back down from the high of being with Tate again. We were always good at this. One thing we got right.

Tate lifted his head and kissed my shoulder again. He tucked my breasts back into the corset and retied the ribbons.

"I don't want to pull out." He sighed. "But wc can't stay here."

I glanced around the bathroom and laughed. Tate laughed with me. He left the haven of my body and gathered a wad of toilet paper. He cleaned me up before dressing himself. I wriggled off the sink and tugged my thong back into place.

"Now what?" I asked.

"I take you home like I should have to start with." He opened the door, then slammed it shut. "Shit."

"That bad, huh?"

It wasn't the first time I'd hidden from eager fans. It wouldn't be the first time Tate had either. The two of us together would cause a riot, especially after being in a bathroom together for this long and coming out looking like we'd just had sex.

"We need a distraction," I said.

"On it." Tate whipped out his phone and dialed. "Bro, I'm in the bathroom with Olive and we need a distraction. Come strut your famous self down here, so these people will swoon over you."

"What's in it for me?" his brother, Conrad, asked, his voice clear through the phone.

"I'll let you drive my car."

"Deal. I'll be there in a minute."

Tate slipped his phone into the back pocket of his costume. Only now did I take the time to examine his green leprechaun costume, which was more a slick, shiny green suit, a button-up shirt, and a bowtie.

I suppose the hat topped off the outfit and made it an actual costume. Whereas mine was most definitely a costume from the tight corset top to the flared skirt that barely covered my buttocks and the striped green and white stockings that reached mid-thigh. Then there were the killer black heels on my feet. They weren't part of the costume since they were from my wardrobe and my favorite pairs of shoes. The tiny hat on my head was more of a hair accessory than anything else.

"I guess your brother is here."

As if to punctuate my words, Conrad's booming voice echoed through the suddenly quiet hallway.

"Hello, lovelies. Yes, I'll sign my autograph for you."

Women screamed. I rolled my eyes. Conrad Saint James might be the hottest actor right now, but I remembered when we'd all hung out at school together in the drama club and everyone else in the school called us freaks. Guess we'd shown them now we were all famous.

Tate cracked the door open again and peeked through the gap. He gave me a quick nod, then slipped out into the hallway. I took a deep breath and walked out of the bathroom, my head high as though I'd done nothing wrong. No one even looked my way. Every person was clamoring for Conrad to sign his autograph. The man had a sharpie in his hand and was signing whatever the women wanted. Even their chests. Would this be Tate's life after he filmed his next movie? Rumor had it the movie would be a tremendous hit with Tate as the lead male actor. Who would they pick for his female co-star? My fists clenched and my jaw tightened at the thought of whoever it was because they'd get to spend time with Tate when I didn't.

A warm hand clasped mine while I'd been daydreaming, Tate came to my rescue a split second before a young woman spotted us. We ran down the hallway as she shrieked our names.

"Damn it," Tate muttered. "I'd hoped no one would spot us."

"Faster." I puffed as I sprinted in the heels praying I didn't twist an ankle at the very least or worse, break one.

We reached the exit and burst through the heavy door. The icy air hit my over-heated body like an artic wind whipping across an ice cap. I shivered, remembering my coat was still inside the bar.

"This way. My car is over here." Tate tugged my hand and slowed to a fast walk when the back door didn't open behind us and the throng of fans didn't follow us.

A dark sedan sat by the sidewalk. Its windows were as dark as the car's paint. A driver stepped out of the car and opened the back door. Tate ushered me inside and snapped my seatbelt in place.

"I can do it myself," I said, tapping his hand out of the way, but he'd already buckled me in.

"Making sure you don't run off on me before we talk."

"There's not much to talk about." I huffed and sunk back into the seat.

Tate dared to roll his eyes. I tugged the hem of my costume down, but it wouldn't cover the gap between my stockings and the edge of the flared skirt.

The driver started the car and set off down the busy roads. I stared out the window, grateful no one would see me leaving with Tate. As if they hadn't already seen me go into a bathroom with him. I sighed. This would be terrible publicity when it got out.

"What's wrong?"

"Someone will leak a photo of us going into the bathroom."

"Conrad will take care of that."

I snapped my head his way. "How?"

Tate smirked. "He's obscenely rich now he's ultra-famous. It's amazing what money buys."

"Lucky him."

"Not luck, babe. He works hard."

"We all do." I tapped my finger on my thigh.

Tate sighed. "I hoped you wouldn't be prickly after an orgasm or two."

"Prickly?" I narrowed my eyes.

"Olive." He slid his hand onto my thigh under my tapping finger. "Please give me another chance."

"You're doing this here?" I jerked my leg away from his warm palm. As much as I wanted his touch, my heart was bleeding a river again. I couldn't have him and lose him again. What was I thinking giving into our chemistry at the bar?

"You're right. I'll wait until we're at my house." He turned to face out the window, putting his fists on his thighs.

I inhaled a deep breath, but all that did was fill my lungs with the heady aroma of the man I still loved. I'd always love him.

The car ride was quiet for the rest of our journey. He didn't even put on music. Which left me with thoughts whirring in my head. Could I give him another chance? Would we make it this time as a couple if I did? The car rolled to a stop, and the driver opened the back door for Tate. He climbed out, then offered me his hand. I unsnapped my seatbelt, slid across the leather seats, and took his hand.

Stepping out of the warm car, the cool night air hit my body again. I shivered nonstop, whether from nerves or the weather, I wasn't sure. Tate unbuttoned his green jacket and draped it over my shoulders. I snuck a sniff of the collar. Tate's familiar aroma weaved more threads inside my head and around my heart.

I inhaled again and lifted my gaze. Before my eyes stood the house of my dreams. A Victorian mansion in all its splendor. Intricate woodwork, painted white, stood out against the pale gray walls. A wraparound porch hugged the cylindrical turrets and the tower roofs. I itched to go inside the Gothic-style house.

"You own this house?" I took a hesitant step forward.

"I do. Come on." He tugged my hand and led me up the stairs.

"This is my dream house."

We paused at the intricate front door.

"I know." He faced me and tucked a flyaway strand behind my ear. "I bought it for you. For us."

"When?"

"I put the first down payment on it with my first paycheck."

"But we'd broken up by then."

He cupped the side of my face with his warm palm. "I never gave up on the idea that we'd be together."

My bottom lip trembled as I whispered, "You didn't?"

"Never," he said. "It's you and me forever, babe. No matter the time I don't see you, I'll always love you with all my heart."

My eyes welled with unshed tears. "But?"

He shook his head. "No but from me. If you'll have me back, whether it be today, then never again, I'll still be here waiting for you."

"My job is in Georgia."

"I'm flying off to the movie location in a few weeks."

"See, this will never work."

"Do you want it to?" He peered into my eyes.

I bit my lip and nodded my head.

"Then that's all we need." He tugged me closer and slid his arms around my waist.

"So we see each other when we can, and that's it?" I placed my hands on his chest to stop myself from snuggling into him. Where I wanted to be.

"If that's all you can offer, yes."

"What about you? What can you offer?" I traced a finger along his collarbone.

"The world."

I laughed. "Too big."

"This house?"

"Yes. And?"

"Me?"

"Is that a question?" I tilted my head to the side and gazed up at him through my lashes.

"No. More a concern, am I enough?"

As I gazed into the doubt in his eyes, it occurred to me that Tate had always been enough. He was the one for me.

"Yes, Tate, I don't want to lose you again."

He let out a long, shuddering breath. I stood on my tiptoes and kissed him on the lips. Our lips danced together so perfectly I knew I'd chosen right. If Tate and I still had this connection after years apart, what was a few months away here and there while filming?

I broke the kiss and grinned. "Are you going to show me around our house?"

"Our house." He grinned back at me. "I love the sound of that."

"I love you," I said. "Always have."

"I love you, too. Always will." He unlocked the front door and led me inside.

The interior was the same as the exterior, just as stunning, with layers, ornate beauty, and eccentric. Like Tate and me and our relationship. This house had stood strong for over a hundred years. Tate and I would be just as strong.

More now we'd found our way back to each other. I wouldn't let him go, and by the pressure of his hand on mine, I had a sense Tate would do anything to hang onto me for a hundred years.

"I have something else to ask you," Tate said.

"Let me guess. You want to have sex in every room?" I cocked an eyebrow.

He chuckled. "Yes, but there's more."

"What?"

Tate's thumb rubbed back and forth over the back of my hand as he said, "The movie production company asked me for people I'd like to recommend as my co-star in the film. I put your name to them."

"Me?"

He nodded.

"You want to do a movie together?" I asked.

"I planned to win you back."

With care, so I didn't club him with my cast, I threw my arms around his neck, and hugged him. His arms circled my waist and pulled me flush against his warm body.

"Did it work?"

I laughed. "Yes!"

Read Hazel and Valentine's story in Lusting After Valentine the second story in the Hollywood Hearts series.

THE LUSTFUL LEPRECHAUN

Read Conrad and Natalie's story in The Lust Bunny the fourth story in the Hollywood Hearts series.

Afterword

Thank you so much for reading The Lustful
Leprechaun.
Did you love my story?
Review it!

A reader who writes a review for a book
is a tremendous gift to the author. It lets
me know that someone read my book and
enjoyed the story enough to tell me. If you
enjoyed this book, please leave a review

on Amazon or GoodReads. I'd be forever grateful.

Acknowledgments

First, thank you to my family for putting up with me disappearing into the world of books. To Belinda, thank you for encouraging me to write again after I lost everything in a computer crash. Remember to back up! A lot of work goes into creating a story, and I'm always thankful for the support of my online writing buddies, beta readers, and fellow authors, Immy for always making me smile, Tammy for believing in me from the start, Karen for being willing to read any level of heat I write. Cassie for her hand holding. Lana for her invaluable knowledge. Also, my fabulous beta reader Erica and her help with US English. The biggest thank you goes to my 'twin' Dannielle, who is the best critique partner, cheerleader, and sounding board ever, and is forever fixing my comma errors, sorry Dannielle I'm afraid you're stuck with them and me. Finally thank you to all you romance readers. You are my tribe.

About Author

Helen Walton is a tea drinking, chocoholic, romance writer. Stories are her obsession. She adores creating sensual romances containing a sprinkling of humor and the all-important happy ending. She lives in South Australia with her family, and menagerie of quirky animals where they all take her away from her book world and demand to be fed. Lucky for them, she enjoys cooking but prefers baking.

Sign up for my newsletter for exclusive content.

https://www.helenwaltonauthor.com/newsletter
Visit my website

https://www.helenwaltonauthor.com/

Follow me

amazon.com/author/helenwalton

bookbub.com/profile/helen-walton

facebook.com/Helen-Walton-Author-1034966677
06602/

goodreads.com/author/show/20249188.Helen_W
alton

instagram.com/helen.walton.author

pinterest.com.au/HelenWaltonAuthor/boards/

tiktok.com/ZSJgrfgrC/

HELEN WALTON

Also By

HELEN WALTON

His Pleasure Contract

Love Negotiations

Her Love Submission

Hollywood Hearts Short Stories

How The Grinch Lusted After Santa

Lusting After Valentine

The Lustful Leprechaun

The Lust Bunny

Anthologies

Reluctant Bride

Alpha Male